Puffin Books

Cal and Ricky both stare at the one-eyed seagull.

'You wanted food,' Ricky whispers. 'There it is.'

'A seagull? You'd eat a seagull?'

'I'd eat anything,' says Ricky. 'Anything.'

When Ricky and Cal wag school they bite off more than they can chew.

At last. Another amazing gizmo story.
From Australia's master of madness.

Other Books by Paul Jennings

Sink the Gizmo

Paul Jennings

*Illustrated
by Keith McEwan*

PUFFIN BOOKS

To Louise and Monique

P.J.

Puffin Books
Penguin Books Australia Ltd
487 Maroondah Highway, PO Box 257
Ringwood, Victoria 3134, Australia
Penguin Books Ltd
Harmondsworth, Middlesex, England
Viking Penguin, A Division of Penguin Books USA Inc.
375 Hudson Street, New York, New York 10014, USA
Penguin Books Canada Limited
10 Alcorn Avenue, Toronto, Ontario, Canada M4V 3B2
Penguin Books (N.Z.) Ltd
Cnr Rosedale and Airborne Roads, Albany, New Zealand

First published by Penguin Books Australia, 1997
10 9 8 7 6 5 4 3 2
Copyright © Greenleaves Pty Ltd, 1997
Illustrations Copyright © Keith McEwan, 1997

Typeset in 12.5/15pt Palatino by Midland Typesetters, Maryborough, Victoria
Made and printed in Australia by Australian Book Connection, Oakleigh, Victoria

National Library of Australia
Cataloguing-in-Publication data:

Jennings, Paul, 1943– .
Sink the Gizmo

ISBN 0 14 038148 1

I. Title.

A823.3

ONE

Is there anyone up there? If there is I'm sorry for killing Ricky. I know we did a lot of bad things today. Well, me more than him. But we both stole the rowing boat. Borrowed the rowing boat I mean. We were going to bring it back. So it really wasn't stealing. And the owner would never have known. Would he?

It was my idea to wag school. It was Ricky's idea to go fishing. It was my idea to borrow the boat. But Ricky . . . Oh, what the heck. It doesn't matter whose fault it was. I've ended up in a terrible mess.

And Ricky's dead.

This is how it all begins.

Ricky and I just pretend to go to school as usual. We give our mothers a kiss, say goodbye and leave home. But inside our school bags there are no books. Instead we have fishing lines, hooks, bait, sinkers, water and food.

'Wagging school is easy,' I say.

'Yeah,' says Ricky. 'All you do is not go. But what will happen at school tomorrow? We'll be in big trouble.'

I laugh like crazy. 'Not a worry. I've already written my note.' I hand a bit of crumpled paper over to Ricky and he reads it out loud.

Dear Mrs Williams,

Please exguse Cal for being absent from school yesterday.
He had a bad cold.
Yours Fatefully,
Sue Rawlins

'That won't work,' says Ricky. 'They know your handwriting. And you don't say "Yours Fatefully". It's *faith*, not *fate*. Fate is about something that's going to happen to you. You can't stop it, and it's usually bad.'

'Well, nothing bad is going to happen,' I say.

'Don't use that letter,' says Ricky. 'They can always tell it's not your mother.' He looks really upset.

'Don't be such a gloom bag,' I say. 'Don't worry about tomorrow. Whatever happens

today's going to be great. A day we'll never forget. And what can they do to us anyway?'

'Plenty,' says Ricky. 'Ground you for two months. No pocket money. No going to the movies. Washing-up on your own for six months. Big lectures for the rest of your life. No ice-cream for –'

'Okay, okay,' I yell. 'If you're that scared, go to school. I'll wag it on my own.'

Ricky stops and thinks about it. I can tell he is tempted. 'Nah,' he says. 'I'll stick with you. After all, we're mates, aren't we?'

I pat him on the back and smile a really big smile. 'We sure are,' I say.

We head off down the road and stop at some bushes. 'Our changing room,' I say. We quickly swap our school uniforms for the old clothes I hid there yesterday. Then I stuff our good ones and Ricky's bag in amongst the leaves.

I reach into the bushes and pull something out. 'Dah, dah,' I say with a wave of my hand.

Ricky grins. 'Awesome,' he yells. He stares at the fishing rods that I hid there two days ago.

'They're Dad's,' I say. 'He'll never find out. What he doesn't know won't hurt him.'

We set off down the road. After a bit the school bus rattles past. Some of the kids in our grade stare back out of the windows. I smile when I notice the looks on their faces. Their eyes just about pop out when they see us walking along with fishing rods in our hands. 'Suffer,' I yell out after the bus.

Ricky and I just about kill ourselves laughing. It is so funny. We don't give a stuff about anything. It is going to be a great day.

'Come on,' I say with a grin. 'Let's head for the beach.'

TWO

My heart sinks as I look along the pier. 'Not one boat,' I say. 'Not one rotten boat.'

Usually there are lots of small boats tied up along the edge of the pier. But today there are none.

'It's fate. We'd better stay here,' says Ricky. 'We'd only get into trouble. And I can't swim. We can fish from the pier instead.'

'You never catch anything off the pier,' I say. 'Everyone knows that. You have to get out into deep water. Where the big ones are.'

We stare gloomily out at the sparkling sea. It seems to be calling our names. 'Rickeeeee. C-a-a-a-l.' The sun is starting to climb and it is growing hot.

Suddenly I see something. 'Look,' I yell. We both squint and stare out towards the horizon.

A tiny speck has appeared, as if by magic.

'A boat,' yells Ricky.

'And it's coming our way.'

The tiny speck grows larger and larger.

'A row boat,' I say. 'I was hoping for an outboard.'

'Boy, he's really rowing fast,' says Ricky.

'For an old guy,' I say.

Finally the boat stops at the pier.

The old man fiddles around for a while. There is a little door at the front of the boat and he is putting something in there. He sure is concentrating – like someone setting a watch or defusing a bomb. He shuts the door and clambers out of the boat. He has no fishing gear. No food.

No life-jackets. Nothing.

'What was he doing out there all on his own?' Ricky whispers.

'He's creepy,' I whisper back. A little shiver runs down my spine. Right down deep in the very back of my mind a little voice is talking to me. It is saying, 'Don't go. Don't take the boat. Run for it. Run for your life.'

I don't listen to the little voice.

The old man doesn't look at us once. It reminds me of when you don't like someone and you avoid their eyes. That is what he was doing to us.

Suddenly lightning flashes. Lightning.

Inside his eyes.

I jump in fright. I swear I jump about a metre. Ricky gasps like a fish that has just been pulled out of the water. The old man has lightning inside his head. Without a word he heads off down the pier and disappears into the distance.

The fibreglass boat sits there. Calling, Beckoning. Tempting.

A one-legged seagull suddenly gives a cry from overhead. I look up and see the blue sky. I feel the fresh breeze. All thoughts about the old man and his eyes and his little door vanish from my mind. 'Let's go,' I shout. 'The boat is ours for the day.'

'I don't know,' says Ricky. 'I don't like this very much. Did you see his eyes? This is weird.'

'Come on,' I say. 'You can't back out now. Don't be a wimp.'

Ricky climbs slowly into the dinghy and I push off. 'Yahoo,' I yell. 'This is the life. Grab an oar, Ricky boy.'

We both take hold of an oar and start to row. Try to row would be more like it. For the first five minutes we just go around in circles. Or fall over backwards when the tip of the oar misses the water. But after a bit we start to get the hang of it and we slowly head out to sea.

Oh, this is fun. This is great. This is really living.

The sun laughs in the sky. The sea chuckles and gurgles. We don't have a worry in the world. Not a worry. The pier shrinks to a tiny line in the distance and finally disappears altogether.

'Let's stop here,' says Ricky. 'We don't want to go out of sight of land. We won't be able to find our way back.'

'Just follow the sun,' I say. 'No worries. The big fish are further out. There's a secret reef.'

'I'm not going any further,' says Ricky. 'It's too dangerous.'

To tell the truth I am out of breath and tired. I couldn't row another stroke if I wanted to.

'Okay,' I say. 'Let's get started.' I take out some whitebait and mussels and start to bait a hook. I drop the line slowly down into the dark, still water.

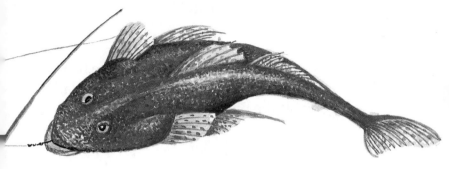

Bang. The line bends over in a curve. 'Got one,' I shout.

'So have I,' yells Ricky.

Soon we are pulling in fish one after another. Flathead. Big ones too.

'Now aren't you glad you came?' I say. Ricky nods. School and Mr Williams and Maths and English seem a long way off. We both have big grins on our faces. Who would want to be in school on a day like this?

THREE

About twenty fish lie on the bottom of the boat. Our lines are in the water, not moving. The flathead have gone off the bite.

'Time to eat,' says Ricky.

We gobble down the cakes and apples that I packed the night before. Soon all we are left with is a large bottle of water. The sun beats down. Hot. Hot. Hot. Sweat runs down our faces like water on a window pane. We gulp the warm liquid greedily. 'Save some,' says Ricky. 'We might need it for later.' I nod and put down the bottle.

'I'm still hungry,' I say. I start to look around the boat. Maybe Lightning Eyes has left some food. Emergency provisions. There might even be chocolate.

I remember the little door at the front of the boat. Something tells me not to open it. But I don't take any notice. I pull it open. There is no food. No water. Just a sort of ball thing.

'Hey, look at this gizmo,' I say. I hold it in front of Ricky's face.

It is about the size of a tennis ball and has little coloured glass windows.

'What are those things on the side?' says Ricky.

'Wings?' I say.

'Nah,' says Ricky. 'They look more like fins to me.'

I put the gizmo thing down on the seat. It looks valuable. Expensive. Not the sort of thing you would leave behind in a boat.

'I don't like it,' I say. 'Why did that old guy leave it here?'

Now Ricky is the confident one. 'I think it's cute,' he says.

We sit in silence. Our lines are still. The water laps gently against the sides of the boat. There is no other sound. Everything is peaceful. I slump down over my oar and close my eyes. Who would want to be in school on a day like this? This is the last thought I have.

Until I wake up two hours later.

Ricky is fast asleep, curled up at the end of the dinghy. The gizmo thing is where I left it. A coloured ball, just resting there doing nothing. The sun is high overhead. My face is stinging. Sunburn. Why haven't we brought hats? Stupid, stupid, stupid. My throat is dry and parched. I grab the water bottle and glug down about ten mouthfuls. I feel better. But only for a moment.

'Hey,' I yell. 'Where's the other oar?'

Ricky jumps up and rubs his eyes. He looks around the boat in fright. 'It's floated off,' he yells. 'Why did you let it go?'

'Me?' I say. 'Don't look at me. Here's my oar. You're the one who let it go.'

We both stand up and stare at the ocean. Not a sign of the oar anywhere.

'Hey,' shouts Ricky. 'Where's the shore? Where's the land? We've drifted out to sea.'

My mouth freezes in horror. My heart seems to stop beating. The ocean stretches out endlessly. We are alone on the empty sea. I don't have the faintest idea where the land is. In panic I grab the one remaining oar and start to row. But the dinghy just spins around helplessly. You can't row with one oar.

Ricky becomes angry. 'Okay,' he yells. 'If you're so smart, let's see you follow the sun. Like you said. Let's see that, eh.'

I look up. The sun is straight overhead. But even if it wasn't I wouldn't be able to find the shore. The sun sets in the west. Fair enough. But which direction is the land? I don't have a clue. Neither does Ricky.

'No one knows we are here,' says Ricky. 'When we don't arrive home no one will know where to look.'

'The kids on the bus will know. They saw us with the fishing rods,' I say.

'But they'll think we've gone to our spot on the river,' Ricky says.

'What about Lightning Eyes?' I say. 'He might know.'

'No way,' yells Ricky. 'If he knew we were going to pinch his boat he wouldn't have let us take it, would he?'

I start to wonder about that old man. Why did he leave that gizmo here? A valuable gadget like that. And lightning in his eyes. He's got something to do with all this.

Think, think, think.

I do think. But only about one thing – water. My throat is dry. I am so thirsty. Very thirsty. The boat bobs and rocks. It seems to be drifting quite fast.

Ricky throws a piece of whitebait into the water and watches as it quickly drifts away.

'There's no land between here and Antarctica,' I say. 'We are going to die.'

We stare at each other in horror.

FOUR

'Stay calm,' I say to Ricky. 'Everything will be okay. A boat will pass by and pick us up.'

'Or run us over,' says Ricky. 'Especially at night. We don't even have a match.'

I think about this for a bit. He is right. All sorts of things could happen. The boat might turn over. There could be sharks. Or worse – a slow, lingering death, dying of thirst and starvation.

Ricky looks at me in a strange way. 'What if I died first?' he asks.

'What are you talking about?'

'Well, you know,' he says. 'You'd have meat.'

'Don't be mad,' I say. I try a little joke. 'You know I hate raw meat.'

Ricky doesn't even smile so I point at the flathead. 'There's plenty to eat,' I say.

'So you don't mind raw fish?' says Ricky.

'It's better than nothing,' I say. 'It'll keep us alive. And if we eat it all we can always catch some more. Don't be a worry-wart. We have everything we need. All we need is what's inside our own heads – our brains. That's all we need.'

'Except one thing,' says Ricky. He holds up the water bottle. 'How long do you think this is going to last? We need more water.'

I look around. There is plenty of water. Salt water. If you drink sea water you go crazy.

And you get sick. And the salt makes you more and more thirsty.

'We can have one gulp each,' says Ricky. 'We have to make it last.' He hands the water bottle over to me. My throat is parched. I take a huge swallow. Then Ricky has his turn. He seems to be drinking a lot. More than his fair share. He puts the top back on the bottle. There isn't much left at all.

The sun beats down. I grab the lunch bag and put it on top of my head. I don't want to get sunstroke. Ricky makes a paper hat too and puts it on his head.

'We'd better rest,' says Ricky. 'We have to save our strength. We'll take it in turns. I'll sleep while you keep a lookout. Then you sleep while I do. That way we won't miss a ship if it goes by.'

Ricky is soon dozing in the hot afternoon sun. My throat is dry. So dry. My tongue is swollen in my mouth. Oh, for a drink. Cool, cool water.

I look at the water bottle lying there with just a few mouthfuls left in the bottom. Way back in the deepest part of my mind a silent voice speaks. 'Go on,' it says. 'Finish it off. There's not enough for two anyway.'

Another little voice answers. 'Ricky is your best friend. Don't do it. Don't do it.'

The first voice comes back. 'He's already had more than you. So what's left is yours. That's only fair.'

'Liar,' I say out loud. I am already going mad. Talking to myself like this.

Minutes pass. Or are they hours? It seems as if I have been lying here for years. I grow thirstier and thirstier.

It gets so that I can't take my eyes off the water bottle. I dip a finger into the sea and lick it. Yuck. Horrible, horrible salt water. It stings my tongue and cracked lips.

Ricky is sleeping. His paper hat has slipped off his head. I pick it up and put it back on without waking him.

'Drink it,' says the first voice. 'Don't be stupid.'

The second voice is silent.

'Quick. Before he wakes up. Drink it.'

Well, why not? Half of it is mine. I could drink my half now. I am so thirsty.

I slowly unscrew the lid. I tip up the bottle and swallow. Oh, joy. Oh, happiness. One swallow of water. Beautiful water. One more, just one more. I swallow again. And again. And again.

No, no, no. What have I done? I have swallowed the lot. My share and Ricky's. I have drunk the lot. How selfish.

I look wildly around. What was that?

It was the gizmo thing. Lights are shining in its little windows. Bolts of lightning flash inside. It has switched itself on. It is humming. Looking at me. It makes a soft whooshing sound. Like the wind. Like the voices inside my head. 'Selfish,' it seems to say. 'Selfish, selfish, selfish.' Is it talking to me?

I have drunk all the water. I didn't really mean to. I just couldn't stop. And the gizmo thing saw me.

What will Ricky say? I don't know what to do. I suddenly grab the water bottle and dip it into the sea. I put in just the right amount of salt water. Ricky won't know what I have done. Not for a while anyway.

FIVE

After a bit Ricky starts to stir. He opens his eyes and licks his lips. His eyes are wide and staring. Staring at the water bottle. The gizmo sits there, all lit up but silent.

'Your turn to rest,' croaks Ricky. His voice is rasping. He is dry and thirsty.

I nod and close my eyes. But I don't sleep. I peer at Ricky through my eyelashes. Waiting to see what happens.

Slowly, quietly, Ricky reaches out for the water bottle. Suddenly he pounces and grabs the bottle. He rips off the top, puts the bottle to his lips, throws back his head and swallows furiously.

In a flash he has downed the lot. Then his mouth explodes in a spray of vomited salt water. He chokes and coughs and splutters. His face is red and twisted.

'You drank the water,' he shrieks. 'You drank it and put in sea water.'

'What about you?' I yell. 'You were trying to drink it all. You're just as bad as me.'

We stare at each other. Ricky looks slightly silly with his red face and paper hat. I have ratted on him. And he has ratted on me. What a pair.

Suddenly the gizmo beeps.

And then Ricky's paper hat vanishes. Just disappears into thin air. We both freak out and stare around us.

BEEP!

Then Ricky yells out. He slaps his hands to his head and starts licking his fingers. He looks up into the sky. 'Who did that?' he shouts.

'What?' I say.

'Dropped water on me,' he says. 'Something dropped water onto me.'

'I wish something would drop water on me,' I say. I lick my cracked lips.

Ricky looks at the gizmo. Its windows are all lit up and little bolts of lightning are flashing inside. 'What's that doing?' he says.

'I don't like it,' I tell him. 'It turned itself on.'

We both stare at each other. Two guilty boys. Both of us had been willing to drink the last drop of water. But I actually did it. I just can't look Ricky in the eyes. I stare down at the fish in the bottom of the boat.

'Beep.' The gizmo is at it again.

'Hey,' yells Ricky. 'Where are the fish? What have you done with the fish?'

I stare down at the bottom of the boat. The fish are gone. And in their place is a pool of water. I drop down and start scooping it up. 'It's fresh,' I yell. Ricky starts scooping it up too. It's like a race, and soon we're lapping at the water. In a flash we lick it all up.

'It tastes good,' says Ricky. 'But where did it come from?'

I nod at the gizmo.

'It must be helping us,' he says.

'I don't think so,' I tell him. 'It doesn't like us. It is paying us back.'

The sun has already dried the last drops from the fibreglass floor of the boat.

'This is crazy,' says Ricky. 'It's like a terrible dream.'

'If only it was,' I say. I look at the gizmo. Worried.

The cruel sun beats down from above. The boat rocks gently. We seem to have been in this boat for ever. It's funny how time goes slowly when you're not having fun. Once again the terrible thirst overtakes me. My tongue feels like a piece of dried cow dung. The top of my mouth is like a tin roof in a dust storm.

Ricky and I slump over. Too dry to talk. And there beside us, blinking and winking, sits the gizmo. The terrible, terrible gizmo.

I stare at the anchor in the bow. Or is it the stern? I don't know. The pointy end anyway. It seems to dance in front of my eyes like a mirage.

'Beep.' The gizmo sounds again.

'Aagh,' I fall back from my seat with a cry. 'Ricky, Ricky,' I croak. 'Did you see that?'

'What, what, what?'

'The anchor. Look at the anchor.'

We both stare at where the anchor had been. It has gone. And in its place is a little pool of water in the bottom of the boat. The sun is already starting to dry it.

SIX

I look at that water. Do you know what is in my mind? I'm not wondering where it came from. I am trying to work out how I can drink it before Ricky laps it up. What a terrible thought. Ricky licks his lips. I can tell that he is thinking the same thing.

Ricky is just about to dive onto the small pool. He looks terrible. His face is burnt by the sun. His eyes are bloodshot. He is stiff and sore.

'After you,' I say. 'Three laps each.'

Ricky gives me a weak smile. Then he falls to his knees and starts lapping. We take it in turns until the whole pool is gone. We both feel a little better. But not a lot.

'Where did it come from?' he whispers.

'And where did the anchor go?' I say.

Another hour or so passes and the sun starts to

dip in the sky. We scan the
sea. Nothing. Not a boat. Not
a whiff of smoke. Not a sight of
land. Only the sparkling, lonely sea.

Ricky's clothes are stiff and dry like the skin of a
dead whale stretched over bleached bones.

'I'm boiling,' says Ricky. 'There's no shade.' He
tries to pull his hot jeans away from his skin.
I watch him sadly. But I'm not feeling much
better myself. This whole mess is my fault. The
gizmo is punishing me for greed. Does it believe in
the death sentence? I can't bear to think about it.

I try to push the horrible thoughts out of my mind. But I can't. Ricky looks hungry. He has a wild glint in his eye. What if he goes mad? Mad with hunger. He might think I am a bit of take-away chicken. What if *I* go mad? That's even worse. I lick my cracked lips – I have never really noticed before but if you squint at Ricky's face it looks a bit like a pizza. Yes, a luscious house-special. His eyes are like olives. And his mouth is like an anchovy. His freckles are like . . . No, no, no. What am I thinking about?

'Beep.' Suddenly my daydream stops. The gizmo sounds again.

Ricky sits there in his underpants. He stares down in horror at his wet, sticky legs.

'Oh, look,' he shrieks. He doesn't know whether to laugh or cry. His legs are covered in cool, cool water. But his jeans have gone. The gizmo has turned his jeans to water.

I try to wet my lips but my tongue is too dry. The water is already trickling down Ricky's legs. I can tell that we are both thinking the same thing. The water is running to waste.

'One leg each,' says Ricky.

I can't believe that I am doing this. But I am. And glad to. I fall down and start licking Ricky's right leg. He does his best to lick the left one. The water tastes of sweat but I'm not complaining. I am so thirsty.

Ricky kicks off his running shoes. 'You can have the feet,' he says.

I lick Ricky's feet. I even suck his toes. I'm not going to waste a drop. No way.

We both start to think.

'Things are turning into water,' I say.

'When the gizmo beeps,' Ricky says. 'It must be helping us.'

'Why would it help us?' I ask.

'Because we're dying of thirst.'

'Yes,' I say. 'But we both tried to drink the last drop in the bottle. We were both selfish. It's punishing us. I just know it. You've got no jeans now. Your legs are going to get sunburnt.'

'But we need water,' he says. 'I'd sooner have water than an anchor.'

'What about the fish? Now we've got nothing to eat. We'll need food too, if no one comes to rescue us.'

'Let's throw it away,' I say. 'The gizmo is bad news. Let's get rid of it.'

Ricky shakes his head. 'It's helping us,' he says.

Just then a visitor arrives. An unexpected visitor. A seagull. It flaps quietly down and sits on the front of the boat.

We both stare at it. A scruffy, one-eyed seagull.

'You wanted food,' Ricky whispers. 'There it is.'

'A seagull? You'd eat a seagull?'

'I'd eat anything rather than die of starvation,' says Ricky. 'Shhh. Don't scare it. We better grab what we can now before it gets dark.'

He quietly moves
towards the seagull.
It seems not to be watching.
Closer, closer, closer.
He almost has it.
One pounce and it is Ricky's.

Suddenly he leaps. And falls
sprawling into the bottom of the boat.

The seagull squawks and flaps into the air in front of us. I stare at it sadly.

The seagull vanishes. Just disappears. A tiny flurry of raindrops fills the patch of air where it had been and then falls like a sun-shower into the sea. Gone without a trace.

'Aagh,' we both scream together.

The gizmo has killed the seagull. Turned it into water.

'If that gizmo is trying to help us,' I say, 'how

come the water fell into the sea? It's not trying to help us at all. It's paying us back.'

'For betraying each other,' Ricky whispers.

'Every time it beeps,' I say, 'something turns into water.'

Ricky becomes serious. 'Cal,' he says. 'We have to stick together on this. If we don't work together we're going to be in big trouble. Everything's turning to water. What will be next?'

I peer around the boat. There isn't much left.

'You're doing it,' says Ricky.

'Doing what?'

'When it beeps. Whatever you are looking at when it beeps. It turns into water.'

'Rubbish,' I say. But inside I feel sick.

'Try it out,' he yells. He throws one of his running shoes over to me and I put it on the side of the boat.

'Now,' says Ricky. 'Stare at it. Don't take your eyes off it.' His voice is shaking with fear.

I look at the running shoe. It is difficult staring at one thing and not looking away. But I do what Ricky says. The minutes crawl by. The sun sinks lower in the sky. But the gizmo remains silent.

'I can't keep this up for much longer,' I say. 'I'm sick of looking at this stupid thing.'

'Don't give up,' pleads Ricky. 'We have to know. This is a matter of life and death.'

Life and death? No way. A nasty thought is trying to crawl into my brain but I keep pushing it away. This gizmo is hostile. Evil. It can do terrible things.

The running shoe
turns into water.
Right before my eyes.
I can't believe it.

There isn't much water in a running shoe. And what there is dribbles down the side of the boat into the sea.

What a waste. I lick my dry lips.

SEVEN

Ricky's eyes are wide and staring. He is terrified.

'It's not so bad,' I say. 'We'll put everything that's left on the bottom of the boat. I'll just stare at it when we need a drink. The gizmo will beep and – bingo! – water.'

'Yes,' says Ricky with a trembling voice. 'But what about in-between times? You don't know when it's going to beep.'

Four beeps. Four at once. Ricky gives a strangled cry. He stands there shaking all over. Naked and wet. His T-shirt has vanished. His underpants. His watch and his earring. They have all turned to water. He stands there without a stitch on.

This can't be happening. It's a nightmare. A terrible, horrible nightmare.

'Oh no,' I shriek. 'You've got no clothes. You'll get sunstroke.' I start to take my shirt off to give to him. After all, it was all my fault. I fumble with the buttons. Ricky needs my help.

'Beep.' My own shirt vanishes.

Ricky is beside himself with terror. 'Get rid of it,' he screams. 'Throw it in the sea. Sink the gizmo.'

BEEP!

BEEP!

BEEP!

BEEP!

With shaking hands I grab the gizmo and throw it as far as I can. It arcs through the air like a cricket ball hit for a six. *Splash*. It lands about ten metres away from the boat.

Ricky smiles. He is still trembling. But he is so happy to be rid of the gizmo.

'Bzz, bzzzzzzzzzzz.' What's that noise? Something buzzing in the water.

Oh no. No, no, no. The gizmo is coming back. Swimming. Its little fins are flapping and whirring crazily. It speeds up to the boat and, like a flying fish, leaps into the air. It settles down on the seat next to me.

Ricky screams and backs away. He scrambles right up to the front of the boat. 'Don't look at me,' he yells. 'Don't look at me.' He is terrified out of his wits. He is staring at me as if I am a monster.

What is wrong with him? What is he going on about? Why is he frightened of me? Suddenly the thought that I have been pushing down in my mind starts to surface. I realise why he is frozen with fear. Too late . . .

'Aaagh . . .'

In front of my eyes. In front of my very eyes. Ricky turns into a pool of water. For just a second he is a water boy. His startled eyes are water eyes. His open mouth is a water mouth. His water arms tremble. And then he collapses. Just like the shower in a bathroom when you turn off the tap. He just rains down into the boat.

Ricky is nothing more than a puddle.

'Curse you,' I shriek at the gizmo. 'Murderer.'

I start to cry. Where the tears come from I don't know. But they run down my face and I lick them. Not that they do me any good. Tears are salty. Just like the sea. 'Oh, someone help,' I sob. 'Bring Ricky back. What have I done? Help. Please bring him back. I'll be good for the rest of my life.'

It's all my fault. I'm a murderer. My best friend is gone because I guzzled all the water. This is a nightmare. Please let me wake up. Please let it be over.

Why couldn't I be the one? Why couldn't I be a pool of water? And Ricky be the one who is left? Bring him back. Bring him back. Someone please bring him back.

I look towards the heavens for help. But none comes. The sky is turning pink. Another hour or so and it will be dark. But the sun is still hot. The air is dry and still.

I sit there for ages. Staring, staring, staring, at the pool that had once been Ricky.

I am thirsty. Oh, so thirsty.

'No,' I shriek at the gizmo. 'I won't do it. I won't, I won't, I won't. I'm not going to drink it.'

I fix my gaze on the few remaining objects in the boat.

'Beep, beep, beep, beep.' They all turn into water. The oar. The bag. The other running shoe. The fishing lines. They all melt into liquid. They form a little stream that runs along the bottom of the boat and blends with the pool that had been Ricky.

There is nothing left. Just me and the boat and the pool. The terrible pool.

I try to push the idea down in my mind. Don't let that thought grow. Don't let it come to life. There's nothing wrong with a thought, is there? It's only *doing* something that's wrong – not the thought. 'Noooooooooo,' I wail at the sky. 'I will not drink my friend.'

I stare out to sea, trying not to look at Ricky's watery remains. What's that out there? Could it be? Yes, it is. Land. I can see land. A small line etched into the ocean. Far, far away, I can just see the pier. I am drifting back to land.

The boat. The boat is all that is left. The boat and me and the gizmo. And a puddle. A deep fear starts to gnaw away inside me. The boat is drifting back. In a way I don't care if I live or die. Ricky is gone. And I can't get him back.

But I want to get home. I want to explain to Ricky's parents what happened. Not that they would believe that he turned into a pool of water. I would just tell them that he drowned. At least they would know where he was.

'You won't beat me,' I yell at the gizmo. 'You won't beat me. I'll close my eyes. I'll close my eyes until we get to the shore.'

But I am too late.

For a second the boat seems as if it is made of ice. Then it collapses. Just melts down into the sea.

The boat has turned to water.

EIGHT

I'm all alone. With only the gizmo for company. A boy's head and a blinking gizmo floating on an empty sea.

I dog-paddle slowly towards the land. I know that I can't make it. It is just too far. And I am weak and tired. And scared.

How far down is the ocean floor? A kilometre? Two kilometres? Ten kilometres? I imagine my body sinking. Floating silently down. Turning and twisting deeper and deeper into the dark water. What's down there? Things that eat you, that's what. Things that nibble at dead toes and eyes. Suck at you with fishy mouths. Pick at you with sharp claws. Strangle you with slimy tentacles.

I am so scared.

Why is the gizmo doing this? 'Stop it,' I shout.

'I'm not really bad. I'm sorry. I'm only a boy.'

The gizmo winks and blinks and circles slowly around me like a tiny shark.

Suddenly my head fills with anger. 'I'll get you,' I scream. 'I hate you.' I thrash and splash wildly towards the gizmo. I want to grab it and tear it to pieces with my bare hands. Or my teeth. Anything. I thrash wildly towards the gizmo but it churns off faster than an Olympic swimmer. Then it stops, watching and waiting.

A dark shape beneath the surface moves swiftly between us. My heart freezes. Let me wake up. Please let me wake up.
Please, please, please.

But it is not a dream. It is real. A triangular fin slices the surface and glides towards me. 'Shark,' I scream. As if there is someone to listen.

The shark is huge. A monster with the power of a train. Its face breaks the surface and I see lines of horrible needles – teeth that can tear and rip. The shark is savage, cruel, hungry. Its beady eyes speed towards me like black bullets. Its fin cuts a smooth scar in the water.

My mind seems frozen, each thought dragging its way through my brain like a pair of lead legs in a nightmare. I have read somewhere that if you poke your fingers into a shark's eyes it will go away. Ridiculous. Stupid. It would be like a moth trying to spit at a roaring truck on the highway. The shark rushes towards me, jaws agape. There is nothing that can stop its onward rush.

I scream and sink beneath the surface, gulping in sea water. My chest seems to explode with pain. I come up and cough and splutter. The sky spins above me.

The shark is upon me. I can see into its dark, dark mouth. Its eyes meet mine.

A wave of roaring water smacks me in the face and tumbles me over like a tissue in a storm. But as I tumble I know one wonderful thing. I have been saved. The gizmo beeped while I was looking at the shark. It has been turned into water.

'Okay, Mr Gizmo,' I shout. 'So now are you on my side? Or do you just beep at any old time? Are you punishing me? Or don't you care?'

Is it just a machine? Set to beep every now and then? Set to turn everything I look at to water? There is nothing else for me to look at. Surely it couldn't turn the clouds above into water. I start to laugh. Loud, uncaring laughter. Clouds turn themselves into water anyway. Clouds rain down all the time. What a silly thought.

Is the gizmo my friend now? No. No it can't be. It is too cruel. Too unforgiving. Ricky and me – we're just kids. You don't kill someone for drinking a bit of water. Or stealing a boat. Somehow I must outsmart the gizmo.

I look at it whirring away a little way off. I know it is evil. That it shows no mercy. 'I still hate you,' I yell.

I float, too weak to swim, looking upwards. A small, white trail is slowly making its way across the pink sky. A plane. For a moment I imagine the passengers sitting there in rows. Their faces glowing under soft reading lights. Drinking coffee. Laughing excitedly as they are carried to far-off lands. Not knowing, not caring that far below a boy floats on an empty sea. Travelling unseen and alone on his final journey.

I stare up at the sky. Is there anyone up there? If there is, I'm sorry for killing Ricky. I know we did a lot of bad things today. Well, me more than him. But we both stole the rowing boat. Borrowed the rowing boat I mean. We were going to bring it back. So it really wasn't stealing. And the owner would never have known. Would he?

It was my idea to wag school. It was Ricky's idea to go fishing. It was my idea to borrow the boat. But Ricky . . . Oh, what the heck. It doesn't matter whose fault it was. I've ended up in a terrible mess.

And Ricky's dead.

I am so lonely. I think of my father's face. Smiling. Caring for me when I am sick. Tucking me into bed. Kissing my head. 'Dad, Dad, Dad.'

The gizmo is slowly killing me. Okay, so I drank the water. I was selfish. But the punishment doesn't fit the crime. I don't deserve to die. Nor did Ricky.

I will never run across the green grass again. Never see a movie. Never eat another chocolate bar. Never ride my skateboard down a hill. Never see another Christmas. Never kiss a girl. You shouldn't die without a kiss. It's not fair.

Angry. That's how I feel. Angry. The gizmo is robbing me. It is me or the gizmo. A stupid, mean, coloured ball. Rage wells up inside me. I will beat it. I will beat it. 'You won't get me,' I shriek.

Bump. Ouch. What was that? Something hard has hit my head. The pain is terrible. Like a blow from a hammer.

I look up. A steel ladder waves above me, reaching up into the sky. I try to make sense of it. A ladder going nowhere. Then I realise. It is a buoy. A rusty buoy with a bell swinging from the top. A chance. Only a chance. But a chance for life.

Think. Think carefully.
Don't let the gizmo ruin it.
I grasp the bottom of the
ladder and then I do the
first clever thing of
the day.

BEEP!

'Stiff cheese,'
I yell out to the
gizmo. 'I've got
my eyes closed.'

BEEP!

BEEP!

BEEP!

The ladder is still
there, solid in
my hand.

'Ah ha,' I yell. 'Got ya,
ya stupid bit of beeping
bulldust. You can't get me
while my eyes are closed.'

I start to climb with my eyes still shut. Up, up, up. As far away from the gizmo as I can get. I count the rungs. 'Twenty-two, twenty-three, twenty-four.' I know that I am a long way up. High above the water. The buoy swings from side to side like the mast of a sailing ship. I start to feel sick.

'Blurgh,' *splash*, 'blurgh.' Oh, yuck. I spew salty vomit all over my legs and the rungs of the ladder. I stare down in hopeless disgust. Is there no end to this terror?

No. There isn't.

BEEP! A tiny sound from far below. And I have my eyes open.

For a moment I am suspended in mid-air. Standing on nothing. Then down I plunge. Down, down, down, like a log plunging over a waterfall. My legs kick as I tumble helplessly in the spray. The buoy has turned into a tower of water.

Spinning, over and over. It can only be seconds but I seem to be falling for ever. *Thwack*. I hit the water with a jolt that knocks the air from my lungs.

I slowly begin to sink. Down below the waves. Down into the deep water. My chest fills with pain. My lungs are at bursting point. I open my eyes and kick my legs. Will I never stop going down?

Yes. Yes. Finally. Slowly, slowly, I float upwards.

Sploosh. Air. Wonderful air. I gulp it down into my heaving chest.

What's that? Small. Coloured. Ball-shaped. Bobbing nearby. The gizmo, spinning in the spray.

I shoot out my hand. Like a frog's tongue snatching a fly from the air.

'Gotcha, gotcha, gotcha.'

The gizmo's fins flap and whirr but I have it clasped firmly in my fist.

'If I'm going to die,' I say, 'You're coming with me.'

But do I have to die? An idea flashes into my numb brain. A desperate plan. It might be the end of me. It might be the end of the world.

I can't be sure. But there is only one thing I do know. It will be the end of my tormentor.

I am going to have to be quick. The gizmo is smart. It knows what's going on.

The gizmo flaps its fins. But they are no use. I hold it high above my head and stare at it. The rotten thing is not going to beep. It knows what I am up to. So, what can I do?

It is going to be a matter of who is quickest. Of timing. And luck.

This is the way I figure it. As soon as it can get me the gizmo will beep. As soon as I fix my gaze on something it can turn into water, it will let me have it. It will beep straight away. Before I can close my eyes.

That's what I think. That's what I am going to bet my life on.

I put the gizmo back into the water and close my eyes. I can hear it whirring around me, swimming in circles.

Now. It's now or never. I open my eyes and stare at my own hand. I can't see the gizmo because my hand is in the way. The gizmo is in the water on the other side of my hand. Quick. If it beeps now I am history. I am water.

Swish.

Quicker than a bolt of lightning I pull my hand under the water.

The gizmo makes its rotten, stinking noise. It beeps. One solitary beep.

And what am I looking at? I am looking at the only other thing in sight. I am looking at the gizmo.

Yes, yes, yes. For a moment the gizmo shivers. Something is happening. The gizmo turns to glass. No it doesn't. It turns to water. A watery ball that grows and grows. It is the size of a football. It is the size of a watermelon and still going. Bigger than a car. Bigger than a house. A huge ball of water wobbling and quivering above me.

It squeaks and squeals. Then it gives a little whimper. Or was it a laugh?

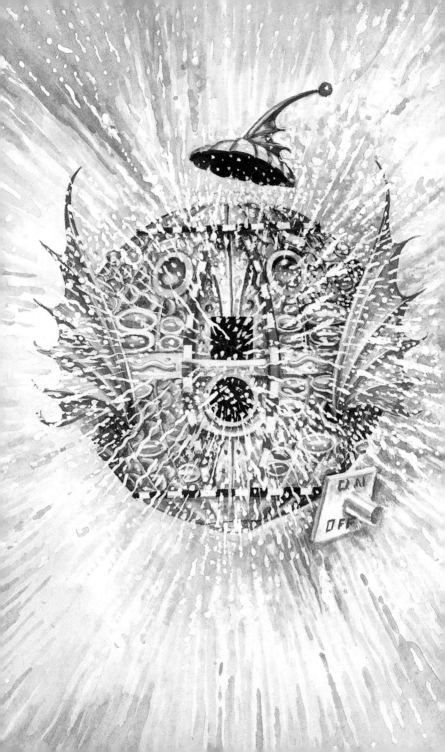

Whoosh. Kerbang. Sploosh.

It explodes with a roar and rains into the air. A huge wave lifts me higher and higher. Then it bends over and dumps me down. The gizmo's last gasp.

I cough and splutter. I roll and tumble. But I am still here.

I have beaten the gizmo. I tricked it. I was too fast for it. I pulled my hand away just before it beeped. It beeped itself out of business. It is gone. And I am alive.

But I am alone. And slowly drowning. I know that I can't last much longer. Every muscle aches. I am cold. I just can't go on. This is the end. But I don't care. I have beaten the gizmo. Now I can die in peace.

Overhead a seagull squawks. A one-eyed, scruffy-looking seagull.

What's this? *Plop*. Something has surfaced from the deep. A running shoe. Would you believe it? A running shoe. A black and red one, just like Ricky's. Then something else. A pair of jeans. What is going on? What, what, what? Is there a chance that I could still get out of this?

Another shoe plops up. Then a school bag. And an oar. Two oars. They pop up out of the water like dolphins.

Soon I am surrounded by the contents of our boat. Has the death of the gizmo released them? The sea is littered with our possessions. The water begins to boil and surge. A huge shape is charging up from below. In the evening shadows it's hard to see. Oh no. Not the shark. Not again.

Not after all this. Please, please, please.
A dark shadow plunges out of the
water and hovers above me
for a second. Then it
smacks down and
showers me with
salt water.

My heart leaps.

For joy.

It is the boat. The boat is back. I swim feebly over and pull myself inside. And there, crumpled in the bottom, is a wonderful sight.

Ricky. And he is alive. He sits up and rubs his eyes. They fill with fear as he searches the boat with his eyes. 'Where is it?' he screams. 'Where's the gizmo?'

'Don't worry,' I say. 'I beat it. It's gone.'

We grin at each other in happiness and fear.

Then we pull on our soaking clothes and start rowing like crazy.

'Did all that really happen?' gasps Ricky. 'Tell me it was just a dream.'

'Two people don't have the same dream at the same time,' I say.

That is about all we can say. We just put everything we have into getting the boat back to shore. We row like devils let out of hell.

After ages and ages we reach the pier. Ricky puts one foot on the ladder and the boat starts to drift away. He has one foot in the boat and one on the pier. Suddenly he slips and falls into the sea.

At that exact moment a dark shape swirls in the water. Oh no, it is the shark. It roars towards us with its terrible mouth open. If it gets Ricky he is dead.

I grab the oar. *Whack.* I smash the end right on the head of the shark and it dives down deep and disappears. Ricky scrambles up the ladder and I follow him.

We are safe.

TEN

So that's the story. That's how I killed Ricky. And after he was dead – well I saved his life. Twice.

So I reckon that makes us even.

As we walk down the pier I look at Ricky and smile. His face reminds me of something and I start to chuckle.

'What are you laughing at?' he says.

'Nothing,' I say. 'I'm hungry. Let's go and buy a pizza.'

Great GIZMO stories

Read them all...